SUGAR LUMP,
THE ORPHAN CALF

Sugar Lump, The Orphan Calf.
Copyright © 1994

by Lynn Sheffield Simmons.

Published by
Argyle Books
710 Old Justin Road
Argyle, Texas 76226.

Printed by
Terrill Wheeler Printing, Inc.
Denton, Texas

Illustrations by Lin Hampton

Title Graphics by Kimberly Simmons

Third Printing, 1998

Printed in the United States of America

Copyright Registration Number TXU 582 976

Library of Congress
Catalog Card Number: 94-72713

ISBN 0-9642573-0-0

DEDICATION

To my mother, Mildred Nelson, who
encouraged and inspired me, and to my
husband, Larry, for all his support.

About The Author

Lynn Sheffield Simmons holds a bachelor's degree in elementary education and a Master's degree from Texas Woman's University in special education. A member of Phi Delta Kappa honorary fraternity, Mrs. Simmons has many years of experience in private tutoring and public school teaching.

A strong advocate of parents and children reading together, her booklets, *Using the Newspaper to Teach Reading Readiness* and *Newspaper in the Home: Helping Your Child with Homework*, have been used in many households. Mrs. Simmons' award winning column, "Up A Creek," historical reviews, and feature stories have appeared in a number of newspapers and magazines throughout Texas.

She resides on a small farm in Argyle, south of Denton, Texas where her husband has a dental practice.

SUGAR LUMP, THE ORPHAN CALF

by

Lynn Sheffield Simmons

Curled up alone in the Texas sand lay a newborn calf. His white face with a black ring circling his right eye stood out against his all black body. "I don't know where his mama is," drawled Ray, the ranch foreman.

"He's so pretty," said twelve-year-old Marcy, bending down to pet the soft, white curls on top of his head, "He needs some milk."

Marcy flipped her long, straight hair over her shoulder as she raced to the house. Quickly she returned with a large baby bottle. She stuck the long nipple into the calf's mouth. He pushed it out turning his head away. She put it back into his mouth but he wouldn't let it stay there. Again, Marcy placed the nipple into his mouth, but this time, she held his jaws as she squeezed on the bottle until warm milk began to trickle down his throat. He made loud gulping sounds as he started to swallow.

He drank and drank until he was so tired he rested his head on the ground. Before he could fall asleep however, Marcy placed her hands on either side of his stomach and began lifting him up. His legs that had been folded up under him stretched out and limply touched the sand, but when Marcy took her hands away he fell. She struggled with his limber body, picking him up as high as she could for his hoofs to touch the ground. As soon as she let go he sank back down. Pushing strands of brown hair from her face she bent over again and pulled his limp body up as high as she could. With renewed strength he strained and stretched his muscles, stiffening his legs until he stood up all alone. As he stood there a big, black dog ran to him and licked his face. "Go on, Bo," Marcy ordered.

When the dog left the little calf began to take a few wobbly steps to follow him, but instinctively, he stopped—and looked at the cows huddled together in the corner of the pasture. His weak, delicate legs hurried to them. When approaching one of the big, black cows she looked down at him, as if she were examining him, and then, tossing her head in his direction she shoved him down. "Get away. We don't want you," she seemed to say.

With much effort he struggled up and ran to a brown and white cow. She pitched her head high in the air and swung at him knocking him to the ground. "Stop it!" Marcy cried out, running to the little calf and hugging him in her arms — thick, black fur, and all.

"I'll take care of you," she whispered softly.

Marcy guided the calf to the cow shed. "You can't leave him out here," Ray said. "He doesn't have a mama to protect him and those coyotes might be back tonight."

"I'll put him in our fenced yard," Marcy said, holding the calf next to her knee as she walked him to the house.

"You'd better ask your mama first," Ray advised, walking beside her.

"I will," she answered, "Do you think he will live if we feed him 2 or 3 times a day and keep him in the yard?"

"I don't know," Ray said, in his deep Texas drawl, "Only God knows that. There's so many things that can happen to a little one without a mama."

After the calf and Marcy entered the yard she latched the gate and went into the house to talk to her mother. "It will be all right," her mother said, "but he'll be your

responsibility and you'll have to be the one to raise him."

Marcy agreed to take care of all the little calf's needs and went into the kitchen to make a special formula. She put into the blender a raw egg, a little honey, powdered milk — especially for calves — and warm water.

After the formula was mixed together Marcy poured it into the bottle and took it outside. When the little calf saw her he scrambled up from the flower bed and grabbed the long nipple with his mouth. Sucking the warm, sweet milk out of the bottle he pulled on the nipple to get more and more. Marcy laughed, "That milk must taste as sweet as you are, Sugar Lump. Hey, that's what I'll name you - Sugar Lump!"

Sugar Lump slept quietly in the periwinkles under Marcy's window, but the next morning when the sun began to rise he started to bellow. "Uuuu-Aaah! Uuuu-Aaah! Uuuu-Aaah!" he bawled until Marcy brought him his bottle.

When he saw her, he rushed to her grabbing the nipple with his mouth. "You like your bottle, don't you?" Marcy smiled.

"What's making all the noise?" asked Marcy's father, stepping outside.

"Sugar Lump, our orphan calf. Mother said I could raise him here in the yard."

"She told me about him when I came home from the city last night," he said, bending down to pet the calf. "He's a good looking calf, but calves are hard to raise without a mama."

"I'm going to take good care of him and he'll do just fine," she answered, confidently.

"If he does, you need to remember he will have to be sold at auction along with the other bull calves, because we only need one bull and we already have him," her father said.

"I know," she frowned, recalling what her father had said the day Ray brought the large bull home from the auction barn.

"He's all we will need to take care of the cows and he will help to produce some fine calves," he had said.

Each day Sugar Lump became stronger and smarter. He ran, he jumped, he

put his head down and kicked his back legs high in the air, and whenever he heard noises from inside the house he would run stand at the door. One morning, Sugar Lump was there waiting for his bottle when he must have noticed the door knob sticking out. Marcy watched from the window as he wrapped his mouth around it. He pulled on it. He tugged at it. He worked so hard bubbles foamed around his mouth and ran down the facing. When Marcy walked outside she began laughing at all the bubbles on Sugar Lump's mouth and those sliding down the door, "Oh Sugar Lump, that's not your bottle that's the door knob!"

One day, Marcy was looking out the window watching Sugar Lump who had taken his stand at the door — waiting —, when Miss Kitty walked up. Sugar Lump lowered his head to watch her walk between his legs. Arching her back she rubbed against him as she marched around his front legs tickling his lips with her ears. Quickly he grabbed one. Miss Kitty sat on the ground while Sugar Lump lightly massaged her ear with his mouth. Marcy started laughing as she watched Miss Kitty peacefully knead the ground with her paws sitting there with one ear in Sugar Lump's mouth. Sugar Lump moved his head back and forth kindly stroking her ear in what appeared to be a pleasant experience for both of them. Then suddenly, quite unexpectedly, Sugar Lump's soft massage became a hard pull. He started yanking and pulling on Miss Kitty's ear until he sucked the other ear into his mouth. Her big, green eyes widened in dismay as she tried to get away, but the more Miss Kitty pulled in one direction the harder Sugar

Lump pulled in the other. He began bouncing her up and down completely lifting Miss Kitty off the ground. Her front paws frantically clawed the air as bubbles lathered around Sugar Lump's mouth and ran down Miss Kitty's face. Hurriedly Marcy bolted out the door prompting Sugar Lump to release Miss Kitty. Sitting there, with both ears dripping wet, blinking bubbles out of her eyes, Miss Kitty squinted a look at Sugar Lump. Then, without hesitation, she lunged at him swatting him with her paw before running up the nearest tree.

Every afternoon after school Marcy and her friends, Holly and Stephen, would take her dogs and Sugar Lump for a walk. Whenever Bo, the black retriever and Tom, the German Shepherd, walked, Sugar Lump

walked between them. If they ran. Sugar Lump ran. If they sniffed the ground. Sugar Lump sniffed the ground. If they ran into the woods. Sugar Lump ran into the woods. Marcy would have to call Sugar Lump back and since she carried his bottle with her, she would give him a drink each time he returned. After Marcy repeated this routine a few times, Sugar Lump began to run to the edge of the woods to hide behind a tree where he waited for Marcy to call him. He would listen for her to shake his bottle before hurrying from his hiding place. One time however, when Sugar Lump ran into the woods and hid behind a tree waiting for Marcy to call him, Marcy and her friends began to laugh, "Sugar Lump, do you really think you are hiding from me?" Marcy giggled.

Sugar Lump was standing behind a tree so small they could see his big ears sticking out on either side.

Later, as Sugar Lump grew bigger, Marcy noticed him watching the other calves as their mothers licked and groomed them. He seemed to long for something he didn't have. Marcy tossed her long, straight hair back as she ran to the house to get the brush she used on the dogs. When she returned she began brushing Sugar Lump. Innately, he stretched his neck up-high in the air for her to rub under his chin and down his throat just like the other calves did when their mothers groomed them.

"Sugar Lump, you are so spoiled," she laughed, brushing one side of his neck and then the other as he turned his head from side to side.

"Hey, why don't you go play with the other little calves?" she asked, putting down the brush and walking him to the pasture.

When Marcy opened the gate Sugar Lump ran toward the calves. Suddenly, he stopped, turned around, and ran back. "No, you stay here to get acquainted," she said, closing him inside.

As Marcy walked away Sugar Lump began to bellow, "Uuuu-Aaah, Uuuu-Aaah, Uuuu-Aaah!"

Marcy went into the house and since she didn't want to distract him from making friends with the other calves she decided not to watch from the window. Instead, Marcy began imagining what was taking place in the pasture. She pictured Sugar

Lump butting heads with the calves —
then, kicking his back legs high in the air
as he ran through the pasture with the
calves following — then, all the cows join-
ing in to be led by Sugar Lump — and —
and she couldn't resist any longer. She
ran to the window only to see that the dogs
had crawled under the fence and Sugar
Lump wasn't playing with the calves he
was playing tag with the dogs.

Marcy called Bo and Tom to the yard
which caused Sugar Lump to start to bawl
again. He bellowed for a long time, but when
he stopped Marcy began daydreaming. She
imagined him running around the pasture
playing follow the leader — then, teaching
the calves how to play hide and seek — and
then, leading the cows down to the pond
— and then — she looked out the window

and saw the calves playing, but where was Sugar Lump? Her eyes searched the pasture. Finally, she spotted him playing all by himself — butting his head against the telephone post. Marcy walked to the pasture and opened the gate. Sugar Lump ran to her and as he followed her to the house Marcy sighed, "Sugar Lump, you're supposed to play with the calves not the telephone post."

"He needs to stay out here," the ranch foreman advised, walking toward them, "you need to start weaning him."

"I'll keep him in the yard while I teach him to drink out of a bucket," she said.

Marcy took Sugar Lump back to the yard.

The next morning instead of pouring Sugar Lump's formula into his bottle

Marcy poured it into a bucket. When she went outside she held the bucket to Sugar Lump's mouth. He bobbed his head from side to side, smelling the milk, but not knowing where to look. Marcy tilted the bucket up to his mouth and let a little milk run out. Sugar Lump became excited and hit the bucket with his head spilling the milk to the ground. Marcy went into the house to mix another batch. This time when she held the bucket up for him, Sugar Lump put his head inside, but soon began tossing his head up and down knocking the bucket to the ground. Marcy returned to the kitchen and made some more formula. She was walking out the door when she saw Ray standing there petting Sugar Lump.

"Are you having trouble getting him to drink?" he asked as he bent down to stuff his pants leg back into his boots.

Marcy nodded. Taking the bucket the foreman placed it on the ground in front of Sugar Lump. Slowly, he reached inside scooping up a handful of milk that he put to Sugar Lump's mouth. He then dropped his hand back into the bucket. He continued dipping up the milk, putting it to Sugar Lump's mouth, and lowering his hand down inside. Gradually, Sugar Lump began following his hand. He put his head into the bucket and sniffed the milk. Marcy and Ray breathed a sigh of relief when they heard him swallow.

"It's going to take awhile for him not to want that bottle, but you keep this up and before long he'll be out there eating with the herd," Ray promised before walking off to the pasture.

"But when he learns to eat grass and hay Sugar Lump will be taken to auction," Marcy thought, sadly.

All of a sudden Ray jumped into his truck and started down the drive. "What's your hurry?" Marcy yelled.

Ray stopped at the fence. "The cows got out of the back pasture and they're either in the woods or down at the highway."

Marcy watched as he drove off. She knew it was serious for the cows to be loose because they could get into all sorts of trouble. One time it took two days to find them and when they did the cows had eaten all of Mrs. Springer's shrubs and left muddy tracks around her fish pond.

Shortly Ray returned. On his way to the pasture Marcy stopped him. "Did you find them?" she asked.

"Yes, they're in Mayor Jenkins pasture," Ray answered, "She said she'd keep an eye on them while I came up here to get some hay. I've got to get them home before I can repair that fence. Sure wish I had a nice, gentle, lead cow."

Hours later Ray drove up the drive honking the horn and yelling out the truck window, "Suuuu, Suuuuu, Suuuuu cow!"

Marcy and Sugar Lump ran to the fence to watch the parade of cows following the truck as Ray led them into the front pasture. Marcy let Sugar Lump out to play as she walked out of the yard to talk to the foreman.

"I was about to think I couldn't get those cows home before dark," Ray sighed, taking off his hat and wiping the perspiration from his forehead with his shirt sleeve. "Once I got them rounded up with a little hay, they would walk awhile and eat, walk awhile and eat, on and on."

"How did you know when they wanted to eat?" she asked.

"They'd stop walking and if they stopped too long I'd have cows all over the place. So I'd feed them a little from the bed of the truck to get them to follow it for some more. A good lead cow sure would have helped."

While they were talking Sugar Lump played with the dogs well out of the view of Miss Kitty who walked up and was sitting

beside Marcy's foot washing her face with her paw. Softly, in the quietest, almost soundless, manner Sugar Lump sneaked up from behind. Directing his head right above Miss Kitty's, he blew a gush of air that made the loudest, deepest, bellowing sound Marcy had ever heard. Ray jumped, Marcy screeched, and Miss Kitty spiraled into the air. "Ouuu-weee," Ray laughed, rubbing his ear as he climbed into his truck and — as Miss Kitty ran up a tree, "he made enough noise to plumb near jump you out of your boots."

After a couple of weeks Sugar Lump was eating grass and hay. Marcy also fed him cow cubes as a special treat whenever he would come to her call. When she rattled the bucket of cubes and called, "Sugar, Sugar, Suuu-gar Lump!"

He would hurry to her and she would give him a handful of cubes.

Marcy knew she didn't have any more excuses for keeping Sugar Lump in the yard and one day she led him to the pasture to stay.

"You're going to be out here from now on," she whispered, hugging his neck and holding back the tears, "I'll be checking on you."

"I know you want to keep him," Ray said as he walked over to her and patted her shoulder, "but you should be proud. You've taken real good care of him and he hasn't had all the sicknesses most orphaned calves get."

"I know," Marcy answered, wiping back a tear as another one fell.

Sugar Lump seemed to accept being with the other cows and began grazing with the herd. Marcy closed the gate and returned to the house.

That night Marcy was awakened by the dogs barking and Sugar Lump bellowing, "Uuuu-aaah! Uuuu-aaah!, Uuuu-aaah!"

Marcy ran to the back porch where her father was turning on the pasture lights. The dogs were growling and running up and down the pasture fence stopping at times to paw the fence, in an attempt to get to the other side, but since Ray had repaired it they couldn't crawl through. Sugar Lump's bawling became fainter and fainter.

"I'll go outside to take a look," her father said.

"What do you think is happening?" she asked.

"Coyotes probably," he answered, walking out the door.

Marcy's throat tightened and tears filled her eyes. "If I hadn't put Sugar Lump in the pasture he would be safe in the yard sleeping in the periwinkles," she thought, rushing to her room. Marcy dressed quickly and ran outside to join her father. He had the dogs tied, but they continued barking as they pulled at their leashes.

"Wouldn't it be better to let the dogs go to Sugar Lump? she asked.

"No, I'm afraid Bo and Tom might scatter the cows more than whatever is chasing them," her father said, shining a big spot light through the woods beyond the pasture. "I don't see the cows anywhere."

"I don't hear Sugar Lump! I'll call Ray!" Marcy shouted, running to the house.

When Ray drove up her father got into the truck. "I'm going, too," Marcy insisted.

"You need to go to bed. You have school tomorrow," her father said.

"Please," she pleaded, "I won't be able to go to sleep."

"All right, get a bucket of cow cubes."

As the three of them drove the roads looking for the cows Ray shined a big spot light out his window while Marcy rattled the bucket and yelled for Sugar Lump out the other. They drove around the roads that circled the pastures, but none of the cows were to be seen.

"We need to get back," her father said, "Ray can look for them in the morning."

"I hear something!" Marcy shouted, "Sugar, Sugar, Suuu-gar Lump! — I hear him!"

She called louder, "Sugar, Sugar, Suuu-gar, Lump!"

Ray stopped the truck as Marcy continued to call and rattle the bucket. Far in the distance they could hear Sugar Lump's throaty bellows. As they got out of the truck Marcy kept calling. Ray and her father cut a hole in the fence.

"He must have broken through two fences to get all the way over here," Ray said, as Sugar Lump's bellows became louder and more constant.

Shortly, the night's silence gave way to the cracking of tree limbs and the rustling of leaves as Sugar Lump noisily approached the fence bellowing, "Uuuu-aaah! Uuuu-aaah! Uuuu-aaah! Uuuu-aaah!"

"Oh, Sugar Lump!" Marcy squealed, hugging his neck.

Suddenly there was more rustling of leaves and the cracking of limbs. "He's being followed," Marcy's father said in a hushed tone.

The three of them stood motionless not knowing what to expect.

"Might be a pack of coyotes," Ray whispered.

The night's silence was again broken by even louder movements coming through the underbrush.

"Marcy, you and Sugar Lump go to the truck," her father whispered, shining the spotlight on the fence.

Quietly Marcy and Sugar Lump slipped away as the noise grew louder. Ray moved to the hole in the fence and held a large stick above his head — waiting. The breaking of tree limbs and the scattering of leaves were the only sounds heard. Ray waited.

Suddenly he threw his club aside.

"It's the whole herd!" he shouted as the clamor of cows approached the fence.

One by one each cow filed through the hole in the fence and walked over to the truck to stand by Sugar Lump. Marcy and her father climbed back into the pick up. Ray began driving very slowly on the shoulder beside the road as Sugar Lump and the cows followed while Marcy softly chanted, "Sugar, Sugar, Suuu-gar Lump."

Every once in awhile Ray would stop for Marcy to reach out the window of the truck to put a handful of cow cubes in Sugar Lump's mouth. When they arrived home Ray parked the truck. Marcy jumped out and fed Sugar Lump some more cubes.

"I'll block off that back fence and fix it in the morning," Ray said, opening the pasture gate for the cows to go through.

"Oh no, you don't go, Sugar Lump," Marcy cautioned, attempting to stop him.

"Why not? It looks like they've made him their leader. Isn't that right, Ray?" her father asked.

Marcy looked up at Ray as he gave her a wink. "Looks to me like they did and he did a real fine job, too."

"You've been wanting a leader haven't you, Ray?" her father asked.

"I can keep him!" Marcy exclaimed as excitement bubbled up in her and she threw her arms around her father.

"I don't see why not," he grinned, giving her a strong hug.

41

When Ray climbed into his truck he chuckled, "I got me a lead cow and you got your Sugar Lump."

When she crawled into bed that night Marcy thought about how proud she was of Sugar Lump leading the cows home and as she was falling asleep she could still see them walking behind the truck following Sugar Lump as she called, "Sugar, sugar, Suuu-gar Lump. . . ."

The End